To my dad

"NO!"

said Rabbit

Marjoke
Henrichs

First published in Great Britain in 2021
by Scallywag Press Ltd,
10 Sutherland Row, London SW1V 4JT

Text and illustration copyright
© Marjoke Henrichs, 2021

The rights of Marjoke Henrichs to be identified
as the author and illustrator of this work
have been asserted by her in accordance with
the Copyright, Designs and Patents Act, 1988

Printed on FSC paper in
China by Toppan Leefung
001
British Library Cataloguing
in Publication Data available
ISBN 978–1–912650–24–8

Scallywag Press Ltd
LONDON

"Time to get dressed," said Mum.

"NO!"
said Rabbit

But that is my favourite top and my trousers with the big pockets . . .

First, Rabbit put his trousers on . . .

inside out,

upside down,

sideways

and the right way round!

And then his top . . .

inside out,

upside down,

sideways

and the right way round!

"Time for breakfast!" said Mum.

"NO!"

said Rabbit

But I can see juicy
orange carrots . . .

Rabbit ate one carrot.
Then another
and another.

Then a little one
and a big one . . .

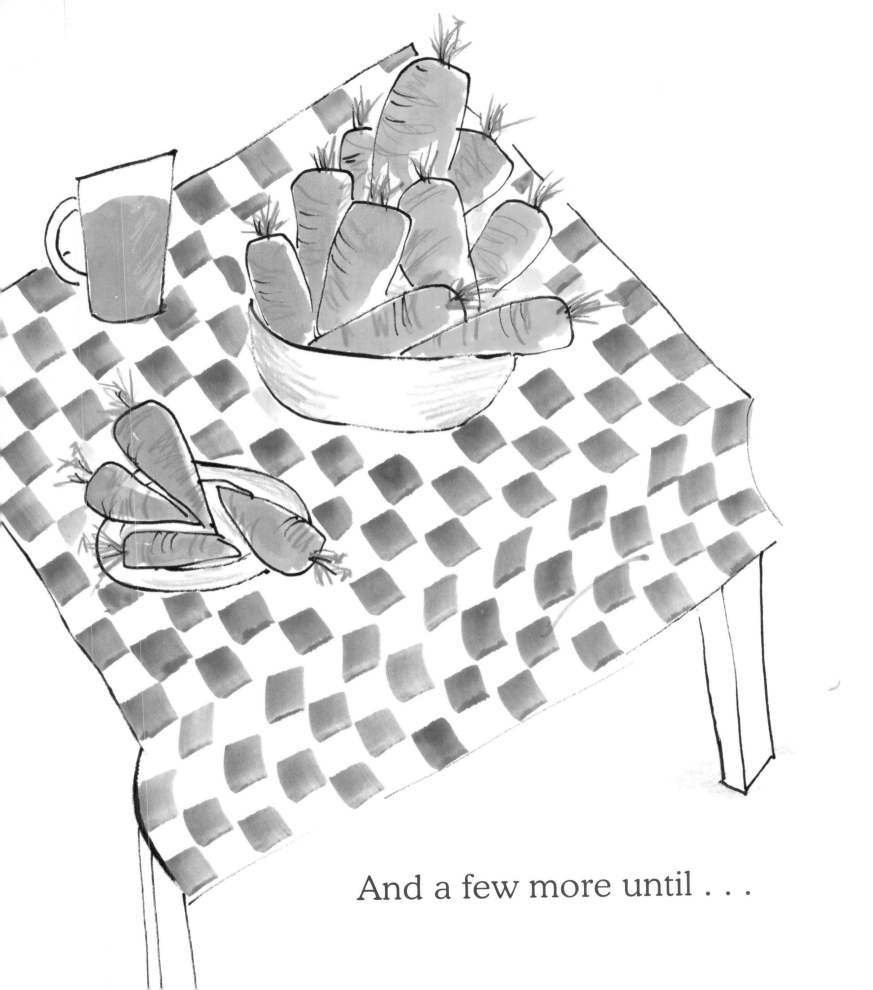

And a few more until . . .

. . . they were all gone!

And then he had a
biscuit or two for
afters when Mum
wasn't looking!

"Time to go outside," said Mum.

"NO!"

said Rabbit

But there
are my lovely
wellie boots . . .

Rabbit put his boots on and went outside.

He jumped in the puddles

and sat in one too!

He cycled,

watered the radishes,

then scored
a goal!

He played
with his kite

and then
his stilts.

"Time for a drink," said Mum.

"NO!" said Rabbit. "I am not thirsty."

"Time for a snack, then," said Mum.

"NO!" said Rabbit. "I am not hungry."

"Time for your potty," said Mum.

"NO!" said Rabbit. "I am too big for the potty."

"Time to go inside now," said Mum.

"NO!" said Rabbit. "I want to stay outside."

"Time for a bath now," said Mum.

"NO NO NO NO NO NO"

"I don't need a bath!"

"But your bath is lovely and warm!"
said Mum. "I am waiting . . ."

"NO!"
said Rabbit

"I am hiding."

"I found you!" said Mum.
"Come with me."

"NO!"
said Rabbit

But there
are lots and lots
of bubbles and
Duck too . . .

"Time to get out of the bath now!" said Mum.

"NO!"
said Rabbit
"I don't want to get out!"
Splosh! Splish!
Splash!

"But it's time for cuddles!" said Mum.

"Yes!"

said Rabbit

"I LOVE cuddles."

"Now, off to bed little Rabbit," said Mum.

"NO, no, no, no . . .

ZZZZZZZZZZ